For Amy, Nina, Don, Cuddles +Teh-bear

# Two Bear Cubs

## Ann Jonas

### Greenwillow Books/New York

Copyright © 1982 by Ann Jonas.
All rights reserved. Printed in
Hong Kong by South China
Printing Company (1988) Ltd.
www.harperchildrens.com
First Edition
10 9 8 7 6

Library of Congress Cataloging-in-Publication Data

Jonas, Ann. Two bear cubs.

Summary: Two adventurous cubs love to wander, but
when frightened, appreciate having Mother close by.
[1. Bears-Fiction]   I. Title.
PZ7.J664Tw   [E]   82-2860
ISBN 0-688-01407-0 (trade).   AACR2
ISBN 0-688-01408-9 (lib. bdg.)

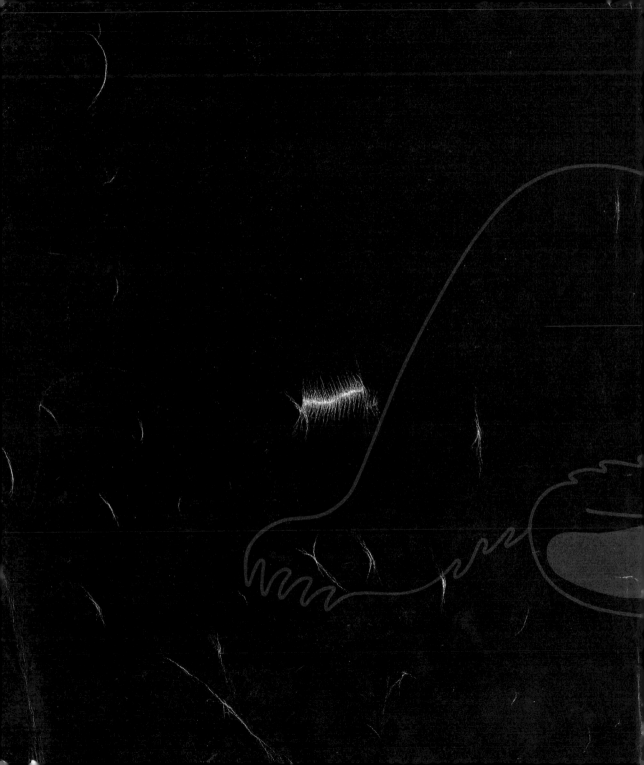

Six bright eyes look out of a dark cave.

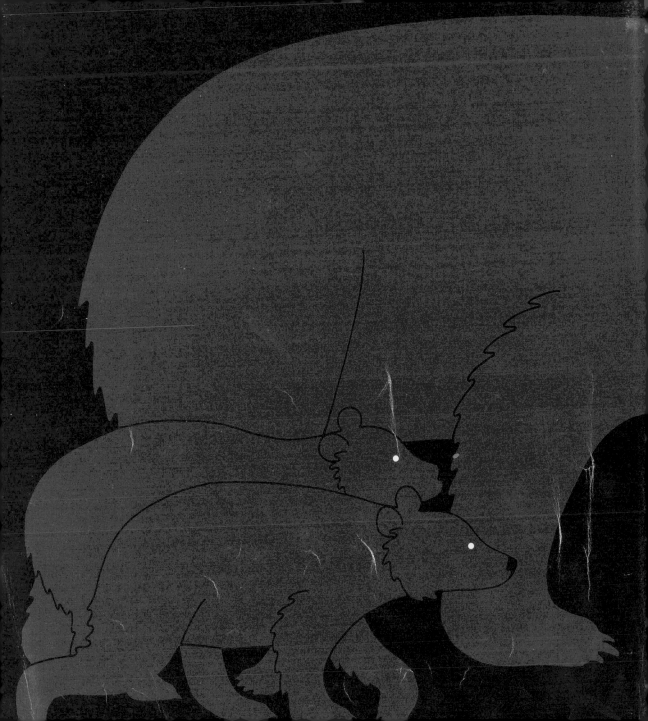

A bear and her cubs begin their day.

**The mother watches while her cubs play.**

**Something walks by.**
**It doesn't smell like a bear.**

**The cubs follow it.**

**It follows them!**

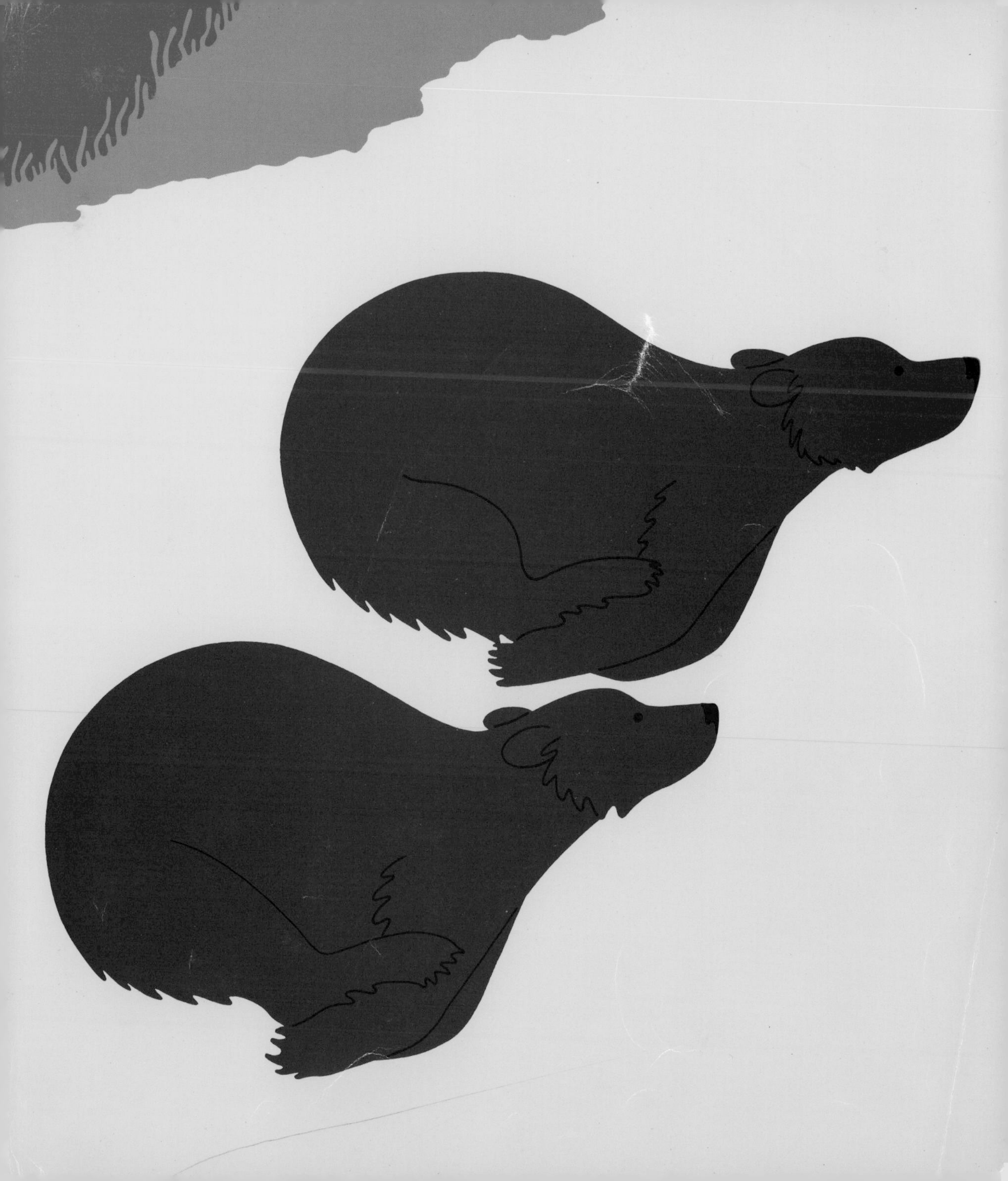

**At last they outrun it.
But where are they?**

**And where is their mother?**

**They look around.**
     **They sniff the ground.**

No mother.

**They find a honey tree all by themselves—**

**and a lot of angry bees!**
**Where is their mother?**

They can't even catch a fish.
Where can their mother be?

There she is!

**And they aren't even very far from home.**